The Railway Rabbits

Fern and the
Fiery Dragon

Collect all the Railway Rabbits books now!

Wisher and the Runaway Piglet

Bramble and the Easter Egg

Fern and the Dancing Hare

Bracken Finds a Secret Tunnel

Mellow and the Great River Rescue

Fern and the Fiery Dragon

Bramble and the Treasure Hunt

Barley and the Duck Race

Wisher and the Noisy Crows

Berry and the Amazing Maze

Bracken and the Wild Bunch

Berry Goes to Winterland

The Railway Rabbits

Fern and the Fiery Dragon

Georgie Adams

Illustrated by Anna Currey

Orion
Children's Books

First published in Great Britain in 2011
by Orion Children's Books
This new edition published in 2014
by Orion Children's Books
a division of the Orion Publishing Group Ltd
Orion House
5 Upper St Martin's Lane
London WC2H 9EA

An Hachette UK company

1 3 5 7 9 10 8 6 4 2

A catalogue record for this book is available from the British Library.

ISBN 978 1 4440 1220 0

Printed in Great Britain by Clays Ltd, St Ives plc

www.orionbooks.co.uk

*For COVERTCOAT at The Launceston
Steam Railway, my inspiration for
SPITFIRE 47512, otherwise known as
The Red Dragon.*

G.A.

Meet the Railway Rabbits!

Wisher Longears

The smallest of the
Longears children,
Wisher has silvery-white
fur and pink ears.
She wears a kerchief
around her neck.

Personality: Quiet and thoughtful, but
with an adventurous side. When something
unusual is about to happen, her ears tingle!
Likes: Exploring, mysteries, her best friend,
Parsley Mole.
Dislikes: People-folk, being the centre of
attention because of her special powers.
Favourite saying: "My ears are tingling!"

Bramble Longears

Bramble is the biggest and bossiest of the rabbits. He has a shiny, jet-black coat, and wears a stripy scarf.

Personality: A fearless and adventurous rabbit, Bramble loves to be the leader and is very competitive.

Likes: Winning races, playing with his friends Tansy and Teasel.

Dislikes: Losing to his brother Bracken, not being the leader.

Favourite saying: "Wriggly worms!"

Bracken Longears

Bracken has pale, gingery-brown fur and ears with black tips. He wears a spotty kerchief around his neck.

Personality: Like Bramble, he loves adventure, but isn't quite as brave as his brother. He's the fastest, though, and always wins races!

Likes: Running fast, working out problems without Bramble's help, his friend Nigel.

Dislikes: Not being in charge.

Favourite saying: "Slugs and snails!"

Berry Longears

Berry has a reddish-brown coat with white tail, tummy and paws. He wears a jacket.

Personality: Berry can always be relied on to cheer everyone up with a joke. He is always falling over and getting himself into trouble.

Likes: Corncobs, jokes and Fern, his favourite sister.

Dislikes: Monsters, especially the beasts that hide in the maze at Fairweather's Farm Park.

Favourite saying: "Creeping caterpillars!"

Fern Longears

Fern has a soft grey coat with fern-like black markings between her ears, a white tummy and two front paws. She wears a daisy chain around her neck.

Personality: Fern is a worrier and often assumes the worst will happen, but she is also inquisitive, creative and good at finding things.

Likes: Stories, singing, hunting for pretty shiny objects.

Dislikes: Owls, rats and any kind of danger to herself and her brothers and sisters.

Favourite saying: "Bugs and beetles!"

Mellow Longears

Mellow has grey-brown fur, a white nose and big, soft eyes. She wears a straw hat decorated with flowers.

Personality: Sensible and well-organised. She loves all her children, but pays special attention to Wisher, who needs extra protection because of her gift.

Likes: Flowers, chatting to her friends Daisy Duck and Sylvia Squirrel.

Dislikes: Silliness, untidiness and the Red Dragon.

Favourite saying: "Silly rabbits have careless habits."

Barley Longears

Barley has black and white fur, and unusually long ears. He wears a waistcoat with barley straws in his pocket.

Personality: A real worrier! Barley cares about his family, and spends most of his time keeping a sharp watch for trouble.

Likes: His favourite look-out tree stump, his best friend Blinker Badger.

Dislikes: Burdock the Buzzard.

Favourite saying: "Oh, buttercups!"

THE LONGEARS / SILVERCOAT FAMILIES

BARLEYCORN LONGEARS
of DEEP BURROW
GREAT ~ GREAT ~ ELDER PARR

|

BUTTERWORT LONGEARS
& POPPY
GREAT ~ ELDER PARR
& GREAT ~ ELDER MARR
LONGEARS

|

BLACKBERRY LONGEARS
& PRIMROSE
ELDER PARR & ELDER MARR
LONGEARS

MEADOW SILVERCOAT
of CASTLE HILL
AND GREAT ~ GREAT ~ ELDER MARR

|

WOODRUFF SILVERCOAT
& MALLOW
GREAT ~ ELDER PARR
& GREAT ~ ELDER MARR
SILVERCOAT

|

EYEBRIGHT SILVERCOAT
& WILLOW
ELDER PARR & ELDER MARR
SILVERCOAT

BARLEY LONGEARS AND MELLOW SILVERCOAT
PARR AND MARR

|

BRAMBLE	BRACKEN	BERRY	FERN	WISHER
BUCK	BUCK	BUCK	DOE	DOE

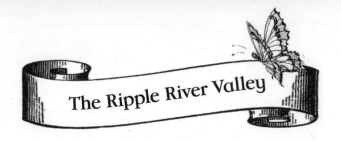

The Ripple River Valley

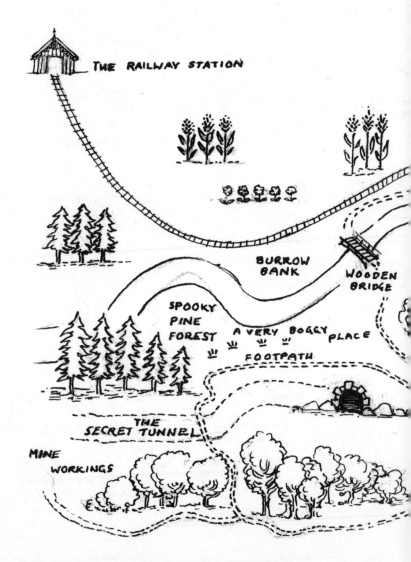

THE RAILWAY STATION

BURROW BANK

WOODEN BRIDGE

SPOOKY PINE FOREST

A VERY BOGGY PLACE

FOOTPATH

THE SECRET TUNNEL

MINE WORKINGS

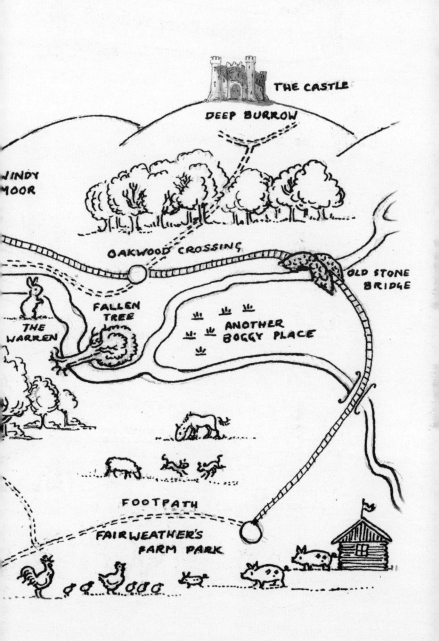

A Hot Day
1

The sun rose slowly over the steeply
wooded hills of the River Ripple Valley
where the Longears rabbits lived. First
Barley, then Mellow Longears hopped
out from their cool, dark burrow into the
bright sunshine. Behind them came three
young bucks – glossy black Bramble,
gingery-brown Bracken and red-coated
Berry. Next was Fern – a doe with soft,
grey fur, just like her marr, Mellow. Fern
turned to look back down the tunnel.

She called to her sister:

"Wisher! Hurry up!"

"Coming!" said a voice. A moment later, a small silvery-white rabbit with pink ears appeared.

"Last as usual," said Mellow with a smile.

Barley twitched his ears, which were unusually long for a rabbit. He was always on the look-out for trouble, especially from his number one enemy, Burdock the buzzard. He glanced up at a telegraph pole where he knew the big bird often sat, waiting to catch his prey. Burdock liked eating rabbits! When he felt sure it was safe, Barley relaxed, just a little. The sun felt warm on his back as he gave his black-and-white coat a shake.

"Another hot day," he said.

"Yes," said Mellow. "Just like yesterday."

"And the day before," said Bramble.

"And the one before that," said Bracken.

"It's been like this for ages," said Berry.

"For EVER!" said Fern.

"Not *that* long," said Wisher.

The rabbits looked around for something to eat. There wasn't much food near their burrow. It hadn't rained in the Ripple River Valley for some time, and the grass was crisp and brown.

"I'm hungry!" said Bramble. "I'm going to look somewhere else."

"I'll come with you," said Bracken.

"Me too," said Berry.

"Wait for us!" said Fern and Wisher.

"Be careful," said Barley.

"Keep together," said Mellow.

They watched the five young rabbits hop towards the big oak. Barley and Mellow were worried. Every day, they had to go further and further to find

enough food. They'd always taught the
young rabbits to stay near home and to
run to the burrow from danger. The dry
weather had forced them to change their
habits.

"It's very hot for the time of year," said
Barley. "I hope it rains soon."

"Maybe tomorrow," said Mellow. She
remembered a saying: "When raindrops
fall, grass grows tall."

Barley's tummy rumbled.

"Just thinking about grass makes me
hungry!" he said. "Let's catch up with the
others."

Bramble and Bracken were arguing.
They had found a store of hazelnuts,
half-hidden between the roots of the big
oak.

"I saw them first," said Bramble.

"No you didn't," said Bracken.

"Did."

"Didn't!"

Normally Bracken tried to please
Bramble. He looked up to his big brother.
But today he felt differently. He thought
Bramble was being greedy. There were
plenty of nuts for them to share.

Bramble glared at Bracken. He was in a bad mood because he was hungry. Besides, he was used to getting his own way.

"All right," he said. "If you want them, come and get them!"

Bracken was worried, but he thought the nuts were worth fighting for. The bucks faced each other.

"Ready?" said Bramble.

Bracken gulped.

"Er, yes," he said nervously.

"Paws up!" said Bramble.

"Best rabbit wins!"

"Ouch!" cried Bracken. "My ear!"

"Ow!" cried Bramble. "My nose!"

From the other side of the tree Berry, Fern and Wisher came running to see what was happening. Barley and Mellow arrived at the same time.

"Creeping caterpillars!" cried Berry.

"Ooo!" said Fern. "Bramble and Bracken are fighting!"

"Oh no," said Wisher.

Mellow was cross.

"Stop it at once!" she said, placing herself between Bramble and Bracken.

"What's all this about?" said Barley.

"I found some nuts!" said Bramble.

"*We* found them . . ." said Bracken.

"Which belong to ME!" said a voice above their heads. It was Sylvia Squirrel, sitting on a branch.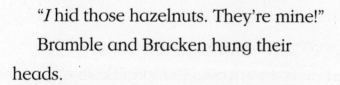

"*I* hid those hazelnuts. They're mine!"

Bramble and Bracken hung their heads.

"Sorry, Sylvia," said Bramble. "We didn't know."

"Yes, sorry," said Bracken.

"I should think so too," said Mellow. "Silly rabbits! Now, make up at once."

"Sorry I hit your ear, Bracken," said Bramble.

"That's okay," said Bracken. "I'm sorry I hurt your nose."

Barley, meanwhile, had been looking at Sylvia's hoard of nuts. Hm! They *do* look good, he thought. Secretly, he wished he'd found them first. Sylvia's voice caught his attention, and he turned to listen.

"Well," Sylvia said. "No harm done. Children will be children, won't they? Such a worry! Always up to mischief and all sorts. But I'm pleased to say I *do* have some food to spare. I've stored plenty of nuts and acorns to last me through winter. Er, if I can remember where I put them! I'm getting very forgetful these days. Please, help yourselves."

"THANK YOU!" said all the Longears.

To avoid any more arguments, Mellow took charge of the nuts.

There were exactly two for each
rabbit and she shared them out. Then
they went on their way.

But two small hazelnuts were not
nearly enough to keep a hungry rabbit
satisfied. Barley, Mellow, Bramble,
Bracken, Berry, Fern and Wisher went
along a hedgerow, stopping every now
and then to nibble at anything they could
find. A dandelion here, a grass stalk
there. After a while, they came to a gate.
The rabbits peered through it to a field
beyond.

What they saw made them gasp with surprise.

"I can't believe my eyes!" said Mellow.

"CABBAGES!" cried Barley.

The young rabbits knew cabbage was good to eat. They'd had it when they'd visited their elders at Deep Burrow. They danced around singing:

"This is our lucky day. Hip, hop, hip hooray!"

Then they all squeezed under the gate.

Toby
Returns
to
Fairweather's
2

Further along the valley, at Fairweather's Farm Park, Fred Fairweather was just starting to feed his animals. The farmer was making his rounds under the watchful eye of Mrs Woolly – a nosy ewe who liked to know everything about everybody. As usual, Fred fed Mrs Woolly first, which she thought was only right because, of course, she was the most important animal on the farm.

"It's going to be another hot day," said Fred, giving her some hay. "I expect we'll have lots of visitors again. People love coming here. Especially to see you, Mrs Woolly!"

"Baa-baa!" said Mrs Woolly, secretly pleased that Fred thought her a star attraction. She watched him cross the yard to feed the geese, chickens, goats and ponies.

Last, he went to the pigs – Agatha
Old Spot and her seven piglets. They
squealed excitedly as Fred entered the sty
with a bucket of food. The fattest piglet,
called Foster, pushed past him to get to
the trough.

"Whooah! Steady!" said Fred.

Shlop, shlop, slurp! went the pigs.

Later, when Gilbert Goose came to see
Mrs Woolly, he found her in the shade of
a tree. She was feeling warm under her
creamy-white fleece.

"Got any gossipy-gossipy-gossip?" said Gilbert. "Any tasty tit-tat-titbits of news?"

Mrs Woolly thought for a moment, but she couldn't think of a thing. Still, she felt she ought to say *something*.

"The train is due about now," she said. "Listen! I think I can hear it coming."

They looked across to the railway line, which ran along the valley. Sure enough, they heard the familiar sound of a train on the track-

Clickerty-clack. Clickerty-click!

They saw puffs of smoke too. Then came a piercing whistle:

Whooo-Wheeep!

The animals at the Farm Park were used to seeing the big, red steam engine, Spitfire Number 47512.

Nearly every day through the summer months, it had brought carriages full of people from The Station at one end of the line to Fairweather's Halt at the other. Today, although the holidays were nearly over, the train was as busy as ever. The unusually warm autumn weather had brought families out to enjoy a day at Fairweather's.

Mrs Woolly and Gilbert watched the train pull up alongside the little platform. There was a squeal of brakes. A *hiss!* of steam. Then it stopped. The passengers came out of the carriages and through the gates of the Farm Park. It wasn't long before Mrs Woolly spotted someone she recognised.

"Hm!" she said. "I see trouble."

"What?" said Gilbert. "Where."

"There," said Mrs Woolly. "Dog! Off the lead. It's the same one that chased Foster the piglet, remember?"

"N-n-n-not T-T-Toby?" said Gilbert.

Mrs Woolly nodded.

"Poor Foster had to run for his life that day," she said. "He was found on the railway line by a little white rabbit called . . . er, let me think . . . Wisher!"

"Oh, my beak and feathers!" cried Gilbert. "What shall we do-do-do!"

"Stop flapping!" said Mrs Woolly. "Go and tell Agatha. I'll keep my eye on *him*."

Gilbert hurried off to the pigs. Mrs Woolly did her best to see where Toby went but there were so many people around that she soon lost sight of him.

As she looked around she saw:

 children in the Play Area

and in the paddling pool,

 a family feeding the ducks

boys and girls
having pony rides,

and a small crowd
around the goats.

Mrs Woolly was a *little* upset that no
one had come to visit her yet.

"Anyway," she said, "I'm far too busy
today. I must find that dog!"

Over by the woods, next to a
cabbage field, Mrs Woolly could see
some campers. She'd overheard Fred
talking about his latest attraction –
The Woodland Camp – so she knew
something about it.

She tried to get a better look. She could see people putting up tents, and children gathering sticks. Hm! thought Mrs Woolly. I wonder what those are for? Then she heard a dog bark. And THERE was Toby!

When Gilbert returned, she told him the news:

"Toby is at The Woodland Camp."

"Good goggly-oggly job too," said Gilbert. "I hope he stays there."

Just then, SPITFIRE gave a loud whistle.

Whooo-Wheeep!

"He's off back to The Station," said Mrs Woolly. "It's time for my morning nap."

Cool Cabbages
3

"UGH!" cried Berry. "I've just eaten a slug!" He pulled a face.

Everyone laughed.

Barley was lying under a large cabbage, holding his tummy.

"I've eaten too much," he said. "I can't move!"

"Me neither," said Mellow.

"I couldn't eat another thing," said Bramble.

"Not even a slug!" said Bracken, looking at Berry.

"It's not funny," said Berry. Then, "Actually, it tasted quite good!"

"Don't!" said Fern. "You'll make me feel sick."

"I *am* feeling sick!" said Wisher.

The sun shone down on the field. It was hot and the rabbits were sleepy. They lazed about between the rows of cabbages where it was cool. Suddenly they heard the shriek of a whistle:

Whooo-Wheeep!

Fern's eyes opened.

"The Red Dragon!" she said.

Fern couldn't see him, but she could picture the Dragon flying along. Puffing smoke. Spitting sparks. She was very afraid of the big, red monster!

"Don't worry," said Mellow. "We're well away from his tracks. We'll be safe here."

"I hope so," said Fern.

Wisher felt sleepy, but somehow she couldn't settle. Her ears had started to tingle – a sure sign of trouble! She looked around to tell someone. Everyone was asleep, all except Fern. Wisher hopped over to her.

"What is it?" said Fern.

"I don't know," said Wisher. "It's my ears. They're tingling. And they feel warm."

"That's because it's a hot day!" said Fern.

"No," said Wisher. "Wait! I can
hear a voice:

Sparks fly! Sticks burn!
The Dragon is coming to
Fairweather's Farm.

"I wonder what it means?"

"Well," said Fern. "Obviously it's about
the Red Dragon going to the Farm Park.
But we know that. We heard him just
now. Maybe you ate too much cabbage."

"You're right about the cabbage,"
said Wisher. "But I think the Dragon
was coming *from* Fairweather's, back to
where he lives at The Station. Anyway,
what about those sparks and burning
sticks?"

"Yes, that is a bit strange," said Fern.

The two sat thinking about Wisher's message, until their heads began to droop and their eyelids felt heavy. Soon, they too were fast asleep . . .

"FIRE! FIRE!"

The loud cries of Fred Fairweather woke Mrs Woolly with a start.

"Wh-wh-what?" she said, blinking in the sunlight. "Where?"

Fred hurried by, talking urgently into his mobile phone. Mrs Woolly ran to the fence and was just in time to catch the words: "Emergency. Fire Brigade. Quick!"

Mrs Woolly looked around. First, she saw the smoke. Then she saw the flames.

"Bah!" she cried. "The wood is on fire!"

A few minutes later, Gilbert Goose flew across from the Play Area into the yard.

"Oh, what a terrible-terrible-to-do-do-do!" he gabbled. "People in a panic. Trees burning. Flames spreading. If they reach the farmyard we're finished!"

Agatha Old Spot looked over her sty. She couldn't see anything wrong and wondered what Gilbert was gabbling about.

"What's all the fuss?" she cried. "Is it Toby the dog?"

"No," said Mrs Woolly. "It's much worse."

She tried to remember exactly what Fred had said on his phone. He had used a word that sounded very important. "There is an EMERGENCY."

Agatha looked puzzled.

"I have no idea what you're talking about," she said.

"There's a FIRE!" said Mrs Woolly. "Fred has called the Fire Brigade, whatever *that* is."

She didn't have to wait long to find out. Suddenly, the air was filled with the sound of a wailing siren. Then through the gates roared a huge, red fire engine. *Ne-e-e-e-nor! Ne-e-e-e-nor! Wow-wow-wow! Weee!*

Gilbert ran around flapping his wings.

"Oh, we shall all die-die-die!" he cried.

Mrs Woolly tried to take it all in. There
was so much happening at once! Some
visitors were being led to safety. The Fire
Brigade ran hoses across the Play Area.
But the hoses weren't nearly long enough
to reach the wood. One fireman shook
his head and spoke to Fred.

Mrs Woolly heard him say:

"I'm afraid we can't get any closer, sir."

"Oh, dear!" said Fred. "There must be something we can do."

He looked across to the wood, then to the railway track close by. That gave Fred an idea. He dialled another number on his phone. Mrs Woolly got closer, trying to hear every word:

"Is that the Ripple Valley Steam Railway?" said Fred. "Good. We need your help right now!"

Mixed Messages
4

Fern woke first. She wrinkled her nose at an unfamiliar smell. A thin mist swirled across the cabbage field. Fern had seen mist before, but this was different. It smelled strange.

"Parr! Marr! Everyone!" she cried. "Wake up!"

Barley opened his eyes, took one sniff and jumped to his paws.

"Smoke!" he said.

"No smoke without fire," Mellow said, trembling at the thought.

"What's fire?" said Bramble, Bracken, Berry, Fern and Wisher.

"Fire is dangerous," said Mellow.

"More dangerous than Burdock?" said Bramble.

"Yes," said Barley. "Even Burdock is afraid of fire."

"But what IS it?" said Berry.

"Flames," said Mellow. "Sparks. Fiery flashes as hot as the sun."

"I saw a fire once," said Barley. "I was just a young rabbit. I'll never forget the smell and sight of it. It started near the Red Dragon's tracks. Flames spread through the dry grass quick as lightning. Everything in its way got burned. Trees. Bushes. And animals who couldn't run away fast enough . . ."

The young rabbits gasped.

"It must have been the Red Dragon's fault!" cried Fern. "He started the fire, Parr. And he's done it again. Wisher's ears were right!"

"What *are* you talking about?" said Barley.

Everyone looked at Wisher.

"Well?" said Mellow.

"My ears were tingling," said Wisher. "I wanted to warn you earlier but . . ."

"Tell us now!" said Barley.

Wisher repeated the message:

Sparks fly! Sticks burn!
The Dragon is coming to
Fairweather's Farm.

"I think Wisher's ears are right," said
Barley. "I never did trust that Dragon."

"Listen!" said Mellow. "What was
that?"

They all pricked their ears and looked
nervously about. The smoke was getting
thicker and hurt their throats and eyes.
They heard the crack and crackle of
burning wood.

"It's the fire," said Barley. "Come on!"

"Wait," said Mellow. "There's
something else. I'm sure I heard a . . ."

Woof! Woof! Woof!

The rabbits froze. It was the unmistakable bark of a dog.

"Oh, buttercups!" said Barley. "As if things weren't bad enough."

"If he comes, I'll punch his nose!" said Bramble.

"I'll pull his tail!" said Bracken.

"It's not funny," said Fern, feeling very frightened. "I don't want to be eaten by a dog."

"I don't want to be eaten by anything!" said Berry.

"Shhh!" said Mellow. "We must run for home as fast as we can. Stay together. Try to look after each other. Remember: sensible rabbits have careful habits! Ready? Go!"

Fern ran along a row of cabbages after the others. She saw Bracken in front. He could run very fast. Parr and Marr were keeping close together, just to her left. Bramble and Berry were running on her right.

She thought Wisher was behind, but when she looked back Wisher wasn't there.

Fern could hear the dog barking. Oh, no! she thought. He's catching up! She couldn't see anything clearly. Fern called to the others. Ghostly voices answered:

"Come on," said Mellow.

"This way," said Barley.

"Keep up!" said Bramble.

"Over here!" said Bracken.

"Hurry!" said Berry.

"Follow me!" said Wisher.

Fern stopped. She looked up the cabbage row. She looked down the cabbage row. But there wasn't a rabbit to be seen. Smoke hung over the field like a cloud. Sooty, black specks fell on her nose and Fern brushed them away. She could hear a distant crack and crackle somewhere over to her left. She thought it must be the fire. It sounded angry. Otherwise, everywhere here was still and quiet. Maybe the dog has gone too? she thought. She hoped she was right. Fern felt alone and very frightened. Suddenly –

"Woof! Woof! Woof!"

Fern jumped. She spun round to face her enemy. The dog was only a few hops away! Her eyes fixed on his pink tongue and sharp, pointed teeth. Then Fern RAN.

She flew along a row of cabbages, darting this way and that way. The dog chased after her. She could hear him crashing through the plants. Oh no! she thought. He's catching up.

Fern ran faster than she'd ever run before. She had no idea where she was going. Now the smoke was getting thicker, and the dog was getting closer. It's no good, thought Fern. He's too fast. When she couldn't run any more, she stopped. Shivering with fear, Fern curled up in a ball and waited for her fate. He's going to eat me, she thought. Oh, I'll never see Marr and Parr or Bracken and Bramble and Berry and Wisher ever again . . .

The dog came up to her, panting.

"Hello," he said. "I'm Toby."

Fern blinked and blinked again. She couldn't believe it. Was the dog friendly?

"I'm F-F-Fern," she said. "Fern Longears."

Then she noticed that Toby was trembling. He looked upset.

"I'm lost," said Toby. "I was walking in the woods with my mistress. Then the fire started! Thick smoke. Hot flames. Blazing trees. Burning branches. I was so scared, I just ran away."

Fern remembered Parr's story about a fire, and the animals that had been caught in it. "You were lucky to escape."

"I'm not very brave," said Toby, hanging his head. " My mistress says I'm a hopeless guard dog. She'll be looking for me. Oh, I hope she's all right. I shouldn't have left her. I must find her, Fern. I was hoping you could help. I saw you over there with some other rabbits. I barked, but you all ran away."

"Y-y-yes," said Fern. She wasn't sure of Toby, yet. "Parr told us never to trust dogs."

"You can trust me," said Toby. He thought for a moment. "Er, I did get into trouble once. I chased a piglet. My mistress was very cross. But I only wanted to play!"

"I heard about it," said Fern. "My sister, Wisher, rescued Foster the piglet. And she was nearly caught by the Red Dragon that day!"

Toby looked confused.

"Red Dragon?" he said.

"Yes," said Fern. "He's a fiery monster! He goes along his tracks puffing smoke and making a terrible noise." She waved a paw at the smoke swirling around them. "The Dragon started this fire. Wisher warned us. Her ears are always right!"

Toby listened. He was trying to make sense of it all.

"The . . . Dragon?" he said. "My mistress brought me to the Farm Park on a *kind* of a dragon. He made clouds of smoke. And he whistled . . ."

"That sounds just like him," said Fern.

"Well," said Toby. "Your Dragon wasn't around when the fire started in the wood. I should know. I was there."

"Go on," said Fern.

"It happened very quickly," said Toby. "I saw some people-folk collecting sticks, so I joined in. I ran off with their sticks and they chased after me. I was having a great time until my mistress called me away. Later, when we tried to come back, our way was blocked by the fire."

Just thinking about it made Toby shiver. He began to whimper.

"I have to find my mistress!" he said. "There's so much smoke I don't know which way to go. Oh, please help me, Fern. PLEASE!"

Fern looked up at Toby. She felt very small beside this great, big shaggy dog. Everything Marr and Parr had told her about dogs whirled inside her head. Never trust a dog. Dogs are nothing but trouble. Dogs eat rabbits! Could she really trust Toby?

Fern felt sorry for him. He looked so sad.

"Well . . . I'll help you, if I can," she said.

Fire! Fire!

5

Wisher reached the end of a row of cabbages and stopped. She had been following Bracken, but he was so fast that she couldn't keep up. She heard Fern call out, but she couldn't see her anywhere. Wisher waited for a few minutes. Then she heard the dog barking again. Oh! I can't stay here, she thought. I hope Fern is okay.

Wisher hopped along a hedgerow, which ran by the side of the field. Spotting a gap, she slipped through and found herself in a wood. It looked familiar and Wisher was sure she'd been here before. But now everywhere smelled horrible and smoky. Then, a little way in the distance, she saw the fire.

Wisher watched in horror as bright, red flames leapt through the trees and sparks flew up like fireflies. She heard the crackle of burning branches, and saw two birds fly out from a treetop. They flapped their big, black wings and cried:

Caw-caw-caw!

Fire spread quickly through the undergrowth, scorching everything in its path. She saw a mouse, a weasel and a deer running for their lives.

She turned to run back through the hedge, but as she did, she felt the ground tremble beneath her paws. At first, Wisher thought it had something to do with the fire. Then, a small mound of earth appeared. And another and another.

Wisher was relieved. She'd seen this happen many times before.

"Parsley makes molehills like these," she said. "I hope it's him!"

She waited by a fresh molehill until a pointed whiskery snout poked through. Two large paws with long claws pushed away the soil, and out popped her friend Parsley Mole.

"Oh, Parsley!" cried Wisher. "It IS you. I'm so scared. The wood is on fire!"

"Fire?" said Parsley, blinking. He was surprised to see Wisher so far from her burrow. "What fire?"

"THERE!" said Wisher.

Parsley wrinkled his nose and looked around.

His eyesight wasn't very good, but he could just see the orange glow from the flames.

"Ah," he said. "That explains the smoke in my new tunnel. Had to come up for air, you see. Can't stand the smell of it. But it's much worse up-burrow! What are you doing here? This wood is near Fairweather's."

Wisher explained what had happened. She told him about the Red Dragon too.

"What makes you think the fire is the Red Dragon's doing?" said Parsley.

"The voice inside my head, of course!" said Wisher.

Sparks fly! Sticks burn! The Dragon is coming to Fairweather's Farm.

"Hm?" said Parsley. "You don't *know* it was him. But we can't stay here! Come on, Wisher. I'll take you home. It's a bit smoky in my tunnel, but we'll be safe. Tunnels are the best way to get about. Up the Burrowers, I say!"

Parsley's tunnel was narrower than Wisher's burrow, but Wisher was small, so she could just squeeze inside.

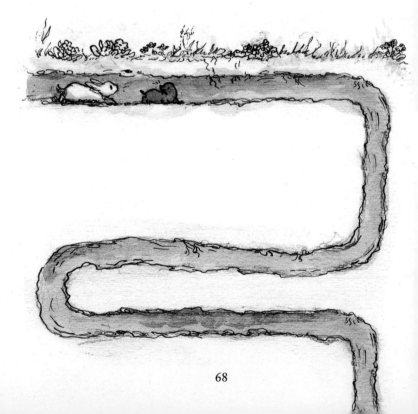

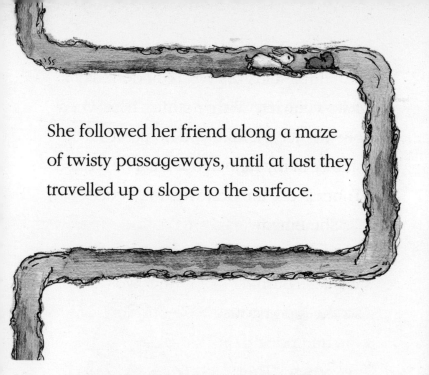

She followed her friend along a maze
of twisty passageways, until at last they
travelled up a slope to the surface.

Wisher hopped out. To her delight,
she saw her burrow nearby. There,
waiting anxiously outside, were Marr and
Parr. Bramble, Bracken and Berry were
there too.

"Thank you, Parsley," said Wisher.

"See you soon!" said Parsley.

"Thank the stars you're back!" said Mellow, giving Wisher a hug. "But where is Fern?"

"I don't know," said Wisher. "I waited for her in the cabbage field . . ."

"Something terrible has happened," said Barley, tugging his ears and pacing up and down. "That dog . . . the fire . . . Fern must have been SO frightened. What if she ran from the dog . . . INTO THE FIRE!"

"Oh!" cried Bramble, Bracken, Berry and Wisher.

"You're making things worse, Barley Longears!" said Mellow. "I'm worrying my whiskers off about her too, but we have to stay calm. Dogs are dangerous. We know that. But most of them are not very clever. I've outrun a few dogs in my time! Fern is a sensible little rabbit. I expect she's hiding in the cabbages. When she thinks it's safe, she'll come home."

"I hope you're right," said Barley.

Fern and Toby made their way down one side of the cabbage field. Fern wondered what Marr and Parr would say if they could see her now – talking to a dog!

"I thought dogs were good at tracking," she said to Toby. "You know, sniffing things out. Can't you use your nose to find your way back to the Farm Park?"

"I've tried," said Toby. "The trouble is, all I can smell is smoke."

"It's horrid," she said. "I can hardly breathe! Let's get out of this field."

In a while they came to a gate. Fern thought she recognised it. They peered through the wooden bars and looked around on the other side. The air was fresher here.

"That's better," said Toby, sniffing. "Where are we?"

"I was here earlier with Marr, Parr, Bramble, Bracken, Berry and Wisher," Fern said. "I *think* my burrow is that way . . ."

She paused. She was desperate to be safely back home. I'm sure I can find my way, she thought. But what about Toby? I promised I'd help him. But Marr said dogs eat rabbits. Can I *really* trust him? Oh, bugs and beetles! What shall I do . . .

"What's the matter?" said Toby.

"S-s-s-sorry," said Fern. "I have to g-g-go . . ."

"Don't leave me!" said Toby, looking scared. "How will I get to the Farm Park? I don't know my way from here. I must get back to my mistress. I wish I hadn't run away!"

A tear rolled down his nose.

Fern gulped. I can't leave him, she decided. She suddenly remembered another of Marr's sayings: "Do a good deed to an animal in need." I wonder if Marr meant dogs too? thought Fern.

"Oh, I promised to help you and I will," she said.

Toby wagged his tail.

"You're a very nice rabbit!" he said.

Fern was pleased. She hoped Marr would be proud of her.

"There's the River Ripple," said Fern, pointing straight ahead. "I can see the little wooden bridge. It's quite near my burrow. And there are the Red Dragon's tracks. If we follow them, I think they'll lead us to Fairweather's."

"Great!" said Toby. "I rode there on the Dragon with my mistress, remember?"

"Yes," said Fern. "You were very

brave! But if we keep clear of the Red Dragon's tracks, we'll be all right. Follow me."

"Coming!" said Toby, trotting after her.

They went underneath the gate.

SPITFIRE
to the
Rescue
6

The cats, Florence and Skittles, were
in the Booking Office of The Ripple
Valley Steam Railway Station when the
telephone rang. Florence had been busy
washing her smooth black coat and
making sure each of her four white paws
was perfectly clean. Skittles, a tabby with
a smudgy nose, had been sitting at his
favourite place by the window where he
could see the passengers.

When the station master, George, picked up the phone, the cats stopped what they were doing to listen.

"Good morning, Fred," said George. "Oh dear! A fire you, say? In the wood . . . by the Farm Park? Yes, I think we can help. I'll get on to it right away!"

Florence and Skittles watched him hurry out of the Booking Office.

"Hm!" said Florence. "It appears there is some sort of emergency down the line."

"A fire," said Skittles. "I wonder how the railway can help?"

"Let's find out," said Florence, giving her tail one last lick.

The cats hurried out to the platform and followed George to the workshop. It was where the steam engines and railway carriages were repaired. They heard a lot of banging and hammering coming from inside. But as soon as the station master popped his head round the door, the banging stopped. John the engineer came out, wiping his hands on an oily rag.

"Trouble at the Farm Park, John," said George. "The Fire Brigade can't reach the wood. It's on fire!"

"Leave it to me," said John. "I'll attach a skip wagon of water to Spitfire. The line runs close to that wood. The Fire Brigade can fill their buckets from the skip. They'll have the fire out in no time."

"Good idea!" said George. "I'll ring Fred Fairweather right away."

"What's a skip wagon?" said Florence.

"It's one of those," said Skittles, waving a paw at an odd-shaped wagon on wheels. There wasn't much Skittles

didn't know about the workings of The Ripple Valley Steam Railway.

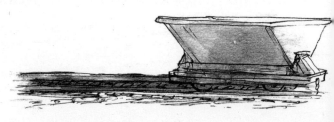

Soon The Station was buzzing with excitement as preparations were made for the big red engine SPITFIRE's special mission. Florence and Skittles sat outside The Station Café, from where they could see and hear everything that was going on. They heard George make An Important Announcement over the loudspeaker:

"WE REGRET TO INFORM PASSENGERS WAITING FOR THE ELEVEN O'CLOCK TRAIN TO FAIRWEATHER'S HALT THAT THIS TRAIN HAS BEEN CANCELLED DUE TO AN EMERGENCY. NORMAL SERVICE WILL CONTINUE AS SOON AS POSSIBLE."

The passengers moaned, but there wasn't anything they could do. Florence and Skittles watched them go into the Café for ice creams, tea and cake to pass the time.

"Look," said Skittles. "John is filling the skip wagon with water from a big tank."

"It takes a lot of water," said Florence.

When it was full, they watched him push the wagon along the rails, then attach it to the back of SPITFIRE. He climbed on to the footplate with Dave the engine driver. The two men put extra coal into SPITFIRE's boiler to get up lots of steam.

"We must get to Fairweather's as fast as we can," said Dave.

"Let's go!" said John.

The signal turned green. George waved a flag. And SPITFIRE gave a piercing whistle:

Whooo-Wheeep!

"Spitfire to the rescue!" said Skittles.

"I hope he gets there in time," said Florence.

They watched the train clatter and rattle down the line until it was out of sight.

Fern and Toby climbed up a steep bank to the railway line. They looked both ways down the track. There were iron rails and stones as far as they could see.

"What now?" said Toby. "It all looks the same to me."

"Y-y-yes it does," said Fern. She was afraid the Red Dragon would come roaring along at any minute. Her heart beat faster and faster as she tried to think. "Let's see . . ."

From where they were standing, they had a good view of the valley. Fern saw the smoke straightaway. It was rising from a wood near the Farm Park.

"It's this way," she told Toby. "I'm sure we'll find your mistress soon."

"*Woof!*" said Toby, making her jump.

For a while they walked along by the side of the tracks. The sun was hot and the ground felt hard beneath their paws.

"These tracks go on for EVER!" said Fern.

She was just wondering how much further they would have to go when she trod on a sharp stone.

"Ouch!" she cried, hopping about, holding her sore paw.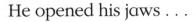

"Are you okay?" said Toby. "Shall I carry you?"

He opened his jaws . . .

"Er, n-n-n-no thanks," said Fern. "I'm fine!"

Phew! I thought he was going to eat me! Fern said to herself as they hurried on. She told herself not to be silly. Toby was only trying to help, wasn't he? But he does have very sharp teeth! She decided to think about her family instead.

"I hope Marr and Parr, Bramble, Bracken, Berry and Wisher got back safely," she told Toby. "The last time I saw them we were running away from you in that cabbage field."

"I'm sorry," said Toby. "I didn't mean any harm. I was frightened too!"

"I know that now," said Fern. In spite of her fears, she believed him.

After following the Red Dragon's tracks round a bend, they saw the wood ahead.

"Look!" cried Toby. "The fire! It's worse!"

Fern couldn't speak. They could hear the roar of the fire. Bright red flames leapt through the trees. Grass and bushes were burned black. The smell of the smoke was awful. Fern wanted to run . . .

Suddenly they heard a noise along the tracks. Something heavy was rattling, clattering, puff-puff-puffing towards them at speed.

Clickerty-clack. Clickerty-click!

Then,

Whooo-Wheeep!

"The Red Dragon!" cried Fern. "Keep back!"

The rails shook under the weight of SPITFIRE Number 47512 as it thundered round the bend, belching smoke and spitting sparks.

The fiery Dragon roared by, blasting Fern and Toby with his hot, steamy breath. Toby barked at the Dragon, to show he wasn't afraid:

"*WOOF, WOOF, WOOF!*"

"Oooo! Don't," said Fern. "He looks angry." Then she thought of Wisher's warning:

Sparks fly! Sticks burn!
The Dragon is coming to
Fairweather's Farm.

But now the message puzzled her.

"There's something I don't understand," she told Toby. "The wood was on fire *before* the Red Dragon came. So how could he have started it?"

"I told you!" said Toby. "The Dragon wasn't around. I was there, remember?"

Fern nodded.

"Maybe I was wrong," she said. "But I still think he's a monster!"

Suddenly they heard the sound of squealing brakes and hissing steam. The Red Dragon was stopping near the wood. They could see people-folk along the embankment and there was lots of shouting.

For a while, Fern and Toby sat watching.

"The Red Dragon is giving the people-folk lots of water," said Fern.

"Yes," said Toby. "They've nearly put the fire out."

"So . . ." said Fern, beginning to understand the real meaning of Wisher's message. "The Red Dragon was coming to Fairweather's to help, not . . ."

But Toby wasn't listening. He had just caught sight of someone he knew. Someone he loved more than anything. Someone he belonged to.

"There's my mistress!" cried Toby.

WOOF, WOOF, WOOF!

Outside the Longears' warren, Barley had decided to organise a search party.

"Fern should have been home ages ago," he said. We must go back to the cabbage field. Marr is right. She may still be there."

"I'll go with you, Parr!" said Bramble.

"And me!" said Bracken.

"Me too!" said Berry.

"Let's ALL go," said Mellow. "The more eyes the better. It won't be easy searching in that horrid smoke." She looked around for Wisher. "Wisher! Wisher! Where are you?"

Wisher had wandered a little way off to think. Her ears were tingling again and she wondered why.

"I know about the fire," she said. "And the Red Dragon. Fern is missing. I know that too. What else could it be?"

Just then, two large birds with shiny blue-black feathers and long beaks flew down. Wisher saw them looking at her with their beady, bright eyes. She felt a little scared, but then they hopped over.

"Er . . . h-h-hello," said Wisher. "Who are you?"

"Craggs Crow," said one.

"Clary Crow," said the other.

"I'm Wisher," said Wisher. "Wisher Longears. I live here. There's my burrow . . ."

Craggs and Clary looked sad.

"We've lost our home in the fire," said Craggs.

"Our lovely-lovely nest gone!" said Clary. "We were so happy there. Now we shall have to start all over-over again. Find a tree. Build another."

"Oh, dear!" said Wisher. She remembered seeing two birds fly up from the burning wood near Fairweather's. "I'm sorry about your nest . . ."

Her ears tingled again. This time she heard a voice:

Sparks fly! Sticks burn!
Seek the Dragon -
and you'll find Fern.

"It's about my sister!" said Wisher.
"I *knew* my ears were trying to tell me
something! Fern has been caught by the
Red Dragon!"

"The what?" said Craggs and Clary.

"There's no time to explain," said
Wisher. "I must tell Marr and Parr.
Goodbye, Craggs. Goodbye, Clary. Good
luck with your new nest!"

"Strange rabbit," said Craggs,
watching her go.

"I hope we see her again," said Clary.

As Wisher
raced back to
her burrow she
heard Marr
calling:

"Wisher!
Wisher! Where
are you?"

"Coming!" cried Wisher.

Back at her burrow she told everyone the message she'd heard.

"Oh, buttercups!" said Barley. "The Red Dragon has caught Fern!"

"Quick!" cried Mellow. "To the tracks! We may be in time to rescue her."

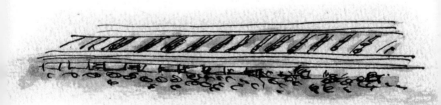

Fern's
Unbelievable
Story
7

Mrs Woolly couldn't remember another
day like it. There was so much excitement
at the Farm Park it was making her head
spin.

Agatha Old Spot called across the
yard from her sty.

"What's happening, Mrs Woolly?"
she cried. "I can't see much from here.
Where's Toby? Is the fire out? Do tell me
what's going on!"

"Yes, yes, Agatha," said Mrs Woolly. "I'll do my best. But it's a job to know where to begin. I can see the steam train . . . I think the Fire Brigade has everything under control. I can't see any flames. Fred looks *very* cross with some campers. They don't look happy at all! There's someone with a dog lead . . . Oh, there's Toby! He's running towards her now. I can hear him barking. And rabbits! A family of rabbits."

Barley, Mellow, Bramble, Bracken, Berry and Wisher hopped to the top of the railway embankment. Wisher looked up and down the line. Something told her which way Fern had gone.

"Come on!" said Wisher.

The sun shone down on the rabbits as they hurried along by the Red Dragon's tracks. The air was hot and smoky. The stones between the rails seemed to shimmer in the heat. All was quiet, except for the sound of a wood-pigeon *coo-cooing* in a tree. The rabbits went as fast as they could. Suddenly Barley stopped.

"Ooo!" he said. "I wish I hadn't eaten so much cabbage this morning."

By now all the rabbits were tired, and there was still no sign of Fern, or the Red Dragon.

"Are you sure we're going the right way, Wisher?" said Bracken.

"Yes," said Bramble and Berry. "How do you know?"

"It's just a feeling," said Wisher.

"I keep imagining all sorts of terrible things," said Barley. "Poor Fern!"

"I'm sure we'll find her soon," said
Mellow.

"My ears are tingling again," said
Wisher. "Look. There's a bend in the
track. Maybe Fern is on the other side."

"I'm glad we've found your mistress,"
said Fern.

"Thank you, thank you, thank you!"
said Toby. "I could never have found her
without you!"

He gave her
a great big LICK
and raced off!

Fern watched Toby run to his mistress. She thought his tail would come off, he was wagging it so fast! Fern didn't want to go too near the Red Dragon so she was glad they had said goodbye from a safe distance.

Suddenly she heard voices calling her name. Fern looked down the line and THERE were Wisher, Bramble, Bracken and Berry hurrying towards her. A little way behind came Marr and Parr.

"Oh, Fern!" cried Mellow, hugging her so tightly she could hardly breathe.

Barley looked at the Red Dragon hissing and puffing on his tracks.

"Well done, Wisher!" he said. "We found Fern just in time. You saved her from the Red Dragon!"

Fern looked puzzled.

"What do you mean, Parr?" she said.

Wisher told Fern:

Sparks fly! Sticks burn!
Seek the Dragon –
and you'll find Fern.

"We thought you'd been caught by the Dragon," said Wisher.

"Well . . ." said Fern, wondering how she would explain about Toby. "I was in danger from that dog in the cabbage field. But he turned out to be friendly! And the Red Dragon helped people-folk to put the fire out. It wasn't his fault the wood caught fire."

Everyone looked very confused.

"I think it's time we all went home," said Mellow. "Fern can tell us everything as we go."

"It's quite a long story," said Fern. "I don't think you'll believe a word of it! I can hardly believe it myself!"

As they set off for their burrow the fiery Red Dragon rattled and clattered down the track. It gave them a cheery whistle as it went by.

Whooo-Wheeep!

The rabbits waved.

Maybe, thought Fern, the Red Dragon is not such a monster after all . . .

Author's Note

The view from my cottage window
overlooking the Kensey Valley, North
Cornwall, and the Launceston Steam
Railway were my inspiration for writing
The Railway Rabbits. The route of the
railway, which runs along this unspoilt
river valley, links the once ancient capital
of Cornwall with New Mills Farm Park
and provided me with the perfect setting
for my adventurous rabbits.

I began my research in January 2010,
by visiting the owners of the railway, Kay
and Nigel Bowman. Sitting in the Station
Café they told me about their railway and
some of the weird and wonderful things
they'd seen, whilst driving the trains.

Yes, Kay is a train driver too! And I rode on the footplate of a bright, red locomotive called Covertcoat, which became my inspiration for the Red Dragon. The idea for the first book, *Wisher and the Runaway Piglet*, was based on a real pig that had wandered on to the line. I'm not sure if that pig was carried home on the train, but it makes a good story!

The stories are told mostly from the rabbit's point of view and, from this perspective, these are big adventures for little rabbits. I've tried to convey a sense of reality about the dangers rabbits face living in the wild – the Longears' number one enemy is Burdock the buzzard. I often see one of these magnificent birds circling overhead, or sitting on a telegraph pole in our meadow.

I hope you enjoy reading all the books in this series as much as I've enjoyed writing them. My thanks to my family and the many people who have helped me along the way. I'm particularly grateful to Kay and Nigel Bowman at Launceston Steam Railway; to Richard and Sandra Ball at New Mills Farm Park; my agent, Rosemary Sandberg and everyone at Orion Children's Books, with special thanks to my publisher, Fiona Kennedy; editor Jenny Glencross; designers Loulou Clark and Abi Hartshorne, and to Anna Currey for her wonderful illustrations.

Georgie Adams
Cornwall, 2014

www.georgieadams.com
www.orionbooks.co.uk

the  orion star

★ ★ ★